DAVID'S SONGS

DAVID'S SONGS

His Psalms and Their Story

SELECTED, EDITED, AND WITH AN
INTRODUCTION BY COLIN EISLER

ILLUSTRATIONS BY JERRY PINKNEY

Dial Books *New York*

Published by Dial Books
A Division of Penguin Books USA Inc.
375 Hudson Street
New York, New York 10014

Text copyright © 1992 by Colin Eisler
Illustrations copyright © 1992 by Jerry Pinkney
Printed in the U.S.A.
Designed by Jane Byers Bierhorst
First Edition
10 9 8 7 6 5 4 3 2 1

Library of Congress Cataloging in Publication Data

Eisler, Colin T.
David's songs : his Psalms and their story
Colin Eisler ; pictures by Jerry Pinkney.
p. cm.
Summary: A selection of psalms, retold, chosen
because they reflect David's life and faith.
ISBN 0-8037-1058-5 (trade)
ISBN 0-8037-1059-3 (library)
1. Bible, O.T. Psalms—Paraphrases, English.
2. David, King of Israel—Juvenile literature.
[1. Bible, O.T. Psalms—Paraphrases.
2. David, King of Israel.]
I. Pinkney, Jerry, ill. II. Title.
BS1440.E57 1992 223'.205209—dc20
90-25459 CIP AC

*The full-color paintings were created
with watercolors. The artwork was
color-separated and reproduced as red,
blue, yellow, and black halftones.*

In my father's memory
C. E.

For Phyllis Fogelman,
for her vision and her belief in me
J. P.

Preface

Of the Bible's many men and women, David is the one closest to life as we know it. Described from boyhood to death as shepherd, singer, boy hero, warrior, bandit, city builder, lover, sinner, and king, his adventures make him unforgettable. Many parts of the Bible tell of David, the New Testament as well as the Old; the prophet Samuel recalls his life at greatest length, and Chronicles gives a more formal account—adding new facts about David the musician, but leaving out others about David the man.

Most memorable of all biblical descriptions of David is the self-portrait given in his own words—the Psalms. Strikingly intimate dialogues with divinity, these prayers are as fresh today as when first sung over two thousand years ago set to David's now long-lost music.

Possibly the son of the king of Judea, David himself captured that title. The Old Testament calls him the Prince of Peace, but for much of his life he was a mighty man of war, winning the lands that later became the new kingdom of Israel. His heir was the wisest of biblical kings—Solomon, son of David and the beautiful Bathsheba.

Jews believe that only a descendant of David could be the Saviour or Messiah, and like that first king of Israel, would be a great leader and healer. So Jesus, born in Bethlehem, David's birthplace more than a thousand years before, won many followers among those who saw him as belonging to David's house and line.

Central to all Christian as well as Jewish belief and service, the Psalms are among the very oldest of all our prayers, standing alone for their intimacy and immediacy. Seventy-three of the one hundred and fifty psalms come with the Hebrew word *Mismor,* meaning that they were to be sung, accompanied by a musical instrument, usually a harp.

Not all of these songs may be David's. Some scholars believe they are a great collection of Hebrew hymns, written over a period as long as a thousand years, beginning five hundred years before David's birth, when the Jews left Egypt in the Exodus, and ending more than five hundred years after his death, following the Babylonians' destruction of David's Jerusalem, an event commemorated in a psalm of dreadful revenge (Ps. 137). Recently, specialists have revised earlier scholarship and credited David for authorship of far more of the Psalms. For this book, only those psalms—and in some cases, only portions—that share the same strong sound were chosen. These are the poems that come closest to David's life and faith. They are presented to recreate a self-portrait in poetry; the lyrical account of a great leader, writer, and visionary, giving his own view of his life, his world, and his God, from his youth to old age.

If this simplified retelling is less magisterial than the original text's, many of the thoughts and words of the Psalms—among the most wonderful ever written—may come closer to the younger reader or listener *now*.

Colin Eisler

DAVID AND HIS PSALMS
Their Story

Long, long ago—so long ago that the Bible, our oldest book, wasn't even finished—a shepherd boy tended his family's sheep in the hills of Judea, where his father Jesse was a leader. They lived in Bethlehem, near Jerusalem. David was the youngest of eight sons, and his name meant "the loved one" in Hebrew. Hebrew was his people's language; their words were used for the Bible.

To find pasture for his flock, David was away from home for days at a time. He wandered in the valleys and hills, searching for fresh water and green fields. David also watched for mountain lions who would try to prey on his sheep. Sometimes mountain eagles swooped down to carry off the lambs, so the strong young shepherd, good at running and leaping, looked to the skies as well as the rocks, for the safety of his flock. He learned how to throw stones to protect the sheep from their enemies on land and above it, putting the littlest lambs in his arms and running fast when danger came.

With only his flock for company, David would get very lonely. He and his sheep could find shade from the sun high overhead among the bold rocks. They often slept in caves at night. Sometimes he felt afraid and was comforted by the thousands of stars shining like little lamps in the deep, deep blue night sky. So far away, yet part of our world, the sky with its magical colors and moving clouds was believed to be God's home and was called the heavens.

In the long, cold evenings, before a camp fire, the shepherd boy would take out his harp and sing. David made up the words and the music for these songs to God. Singing them made him feel safe and gave him courage. He often praised the Lord, thanking him for all his wonderful works, for making golden sunsets, silvery stars, strong mountains, gentle valleys, flowing waters, rich harvests, and healthy children. Seeing the beauty of all God had made, David made joyous sounds with his voice and harp. "Happy" is the first word of the opening psalm. In Psalm 16 David's "heart and his spirit are happy in God's presence . . . [God] with pleasures forevermore held in His right hand," giving David "the fullness of joy." And good people are told to "shout for joy before the Lord" in the opening line of Psalm 33.

All these songs to God are now called David's Psalms or prayers. Singing, David did not feel alone, his words expressing just how he felt, telling what he needed, thanking the Lord for the laws He gave to Moses, the Command-

ments to live by. David often told God just what He ought to be doing for him—helping look after his sheep, providing food, water, and shelter for all, and later, punishing his enemies. Soon God came to David's aid. When the young shepherd went to kill the giant Goliath, an enemy of his people, David had only a slingshot and a smooth stone in his hand. But with God's help the stone hit Goliath in the middle of his forehead and his huge body fell dead at David's feet.

King Saul had David come to his court, where the boy's playing and singing made the sad, moody monarch a much happier man. Soon all the people at court loved him too, for his music and for his bravery. He had become a great warrior, winning battles as easily as he won friends. Saul gave him his daughter Michal in marriage. David and the king's son Jonathan were the closest of friends.

But then the king came to be very jealous of David. He even tried to kill him. David fled, but he had nowhere to go. His parents had lost their lands to enemies of Judea, so David became a bandit. Soon, with his own men he threw out the invaders so that his mother and father could go back to their home, and David became the ruler of Judea.

After Saul's death David became the next king of Israel, and chose Jerusalem, in the land of Zion, as the new capital for the new nation of Israel, for which David had fought, bringing together many defeated kingdoms to make his own. David was so proud of having won the Ark, a religious treasure, back from his enemies, that he danced in the streets. His wife told him angrily, that was no way for a king to behave! Unlike Noah's, this Ark was a beautiful box that kept two stones carved with the Ten Commandments, the laws given to Moses. David or his son Solomon saw to it that the Ark was given a splendid new setting in Jerusalem's new temple.

Though he loved God's laws, the Ten Commandments and other rules, David couldn't keep them. He often confessed in song to his own sins—his envy and meanness, describing his weaknesses just as openly as he did his faith and strength. That's what make his words mean so much, there's always a real person speaking, someone whose words one can believe.

Singing of his life, David seldom says just what happened, not even about Goliath, his worst enemy, or of those he loved the most—unless those poems are lost. Instead, he tells of his feelings over a long life, so we know just what it was like to go through so many adventures, to care, and hate and fear and fight and love over the many years that took him from the lowest to the highest labors in the land of Israel.

David was a poet, giving each psalm a special sense of finding just the right word. "Glory" is one of his favorites. It means shining like the sun, but is also a way of saying great and wonderful. What did David mean when he sang of his heart or soul? These are special places where what we feel and think and believe come together, making us who we are and no one else. You can't touch or see these places—there our love and hope and need, the wish to make and give, to share and thank, are clearest. Faults are there too, in the heart and soul or spirit, the bad right along with the good—everyone with lots of both.

David prayed for forgiveness, for understanding, asking God to save him from sin, from selfishness and dishonesty, keeping him as close to the Lord's rules as he could be. Often cruel, David could also be loving and patient, a father who never believed his son Absalom could want to steal his kingdom and turn his people against him.

A great warrior, a king, and much later, an old, lonely, and bitter man, David sang of troubles and sorrows as well as of victories and joys, telling God of his defeats and sicknesses, his anger and his rage, about people who treated him badly, of liars and cheats.

Some of these psalms are full of hate, of war, of wanting to get even, sung long after that great day, when the young shepherd, with only a slingshot in his hand, killed the feared giant Goliath, that terrible enemy of his people. Then the boy had only sung for strength, for help and courage.

David's words are found in the Bible, now often set to new music because all of his own is long lost. We can share the shepherd boy's love of the beauty of the land, his hopes to become a better person, his thanks for all the wonders of this world. Today if we, like David, want to talk to God, trying to find just the right words for our deepest feelings, those of need and fear as well as of hope, love, and thanks, what we say is often just what David did. His words are sung or spoken in temples, churches, and in our own homes. We often recite the Psalms before going to bed. First sung so long ago, they still help us, as they did David, on our way through day and night.

His songs can also be read as poetry, just for the beauty of their words, for the strength of their lines. They bring us close to sharing the life as well as the work of one of the world's most wonderful writers, whose art is as fresh and new today as it was when first written down three thousand years ago.

THE PSALMS
A Selection

One of the young shepherd's strongest and happiest songs
tells just why he loves God and how God loves him.

The Lord is my light and will save me.
So who can I fear?
The Lord is my shelter.
So what can I be afraid of?
Only one thing do I ask of God.
One thing do I want.
That I may always live in the Lord's house
all the days of my life,

to look upon his beauty
and find God in his temple
where he will keep me safe,
under his roof,
in times of trouble.
He will hide me in his tent
and raise me out of harm's way.
Now I can lift my head up high
over the enemies all around me.
So I sing a song of praise to the Lord.

Psalm 27

Some of David's songs can only have been those of a
very young, unusually strong man. This psalm combines the
wisdom of age and the strong poetry of youth:

If I lift up my eyes to the hills,
where shall I find help?
Help comes only from the Lord,
maker of heaven and earth.
How could he let your foot stumble?
How could he, your guard, sleep?
The guardian of Israel
never slumbers, never sleeps.
The Lord is your guard,
ever the defender:

The sun will not strike you by day,
nor the moon at night.
The Lord will keep you from all evil;
he will protect you, body and soul.
The Lord will guard your going and your coming,
now and forevermore.

Psalm 121

Brought up in the fertile hills of Bethlehem, David was close to farm life. So rich were the wheat harvests there that the town's name, in Hebrew, means The House of Bread. That's why the words and works of the field, of sowing and reaping, are often found in the Psalms.

Turn once again our fortune, Lord,
as streams return in the dry south.
Those who sow seed in tears
shall reap with songs of joy.
A man may go out weeping with his bag of seed;
but he will come back with songs of joy,
carrying home his sheaves of wheat.

Psalm 126

Near the wonders of the shepherd's world, and to the beauty of the word, David's songs go to the forests and the plains to tell of God's strength.

The voice of the Lord breaks the cedars,
the Lord splinters the cedars of Lebanon.
He makes Lebanon skip like a calf,
Sirion like a wild young ox.
The voice of the Lord makes the hinds calve
and brings kids early to birth.

Psalm 29

One of David's Psalms tells of the happy man chosen by God to live in His house, another way of describing the wonderful world He made to be shared by all of us.

Let us enjoy the blessing of your house,
your holy temple.
Fix the mountains in their place,
calm the seas and their raging waves.
You visit the earth and give it abundance,
often enriching it with the waters of heaven,
flowing in their channels,
providing us with rain,
watering the earth's furrows, leveling its ridges,
softening it with showers and blessing its growth.
You crown the year with your good gifts
and the palm trees drip with sweet juice.
The wild pastures are blessed with riches
and the hills encircled in happiness.

The meadows are clothed with sheep
and the valleys robed in corn,
so that they shout, they burst into song.

Psalm 65

One of David's finest poems tells about the beauties of
the skies.

The heavens speak of God's glory,
the curved skies show his handiwork.
The days talk to one another,
the nights share their knowledge.
Without word, speech, or sound,
their music goes through all the earth,
their words reach to the end of the world.

Psalm 19

From his shepherd days, scanning the skies to learn of
the next day's weather, or to find out just where he was,
David was as close to the heavens as a painter of skies, or a
poet, or an astronomer.

When I look up at your heavens, the work of your fingers,
where you have set the moon and stars in their place:
What are we that you should remember us?
Who are we that you should care for us?

Yet you have made us just a little less than gods,
crowning us with glory and honor.
You have made us master of all your animals,
placing all else below us,
all sheep and oxen, all the wild beasts,
the birds in the air and the fish in the sea,
and all that moves in the ocean's paths.

Psalm 8

Singing of Israel's enemies, David even thought of them
as a gardener might view weeds or crabgrass.

Often since I was young have men attacked me—
but never have they won.
They lashed my back with whips,
like ploughmen driving long furrows.
Yet the Lord in his justice
has cut me loose from the bonds of the wicked.
Let all enemies of Zion
be thrown back in shame:
Let them be like grass growing on the roof,
which dries up before it can grow,
and never fills a mower's hand,
nor yields an armful to the harvester.

Psalm 129

He could write about people as if they were beautiful buildings, and he praised the best of days as being those with the rich harvests.

Happy are we whose grown young sons
stand like tall towers,
our daughters like sculpted pillars,
at the corners of a palace.
Our barns are full and will store much food.
Our sheep bear thousands and thousands of lambs.
The oxen in our fields are fat and sleek.
Happy are such people as we,
happy the people who have our Lord for their God.

Psalm 144

We can't live without water. Farmers and shepherds know this better than anyone else. So the young David expressed this in song.

God made the springs burst out of the gullies,
so that their waters run between the hills.
The wild animals all drink from them,
the wild asses quench their thirst,
the birds nest on their banks
and sing among the leaves.
From your high pavilion you water the hills,
the earth enriched by your care.

20

You make the grass grow for cattle
and green things for those animals
who work for us,
bringing bread out of the earth
and wine to make us happy,
oil to make our faces shine,
bread to sustain our strength.

Psalm 104

One of David's songs compares his early labors as a young shepherd to his later life as king. He describes how

God took him from the sheepfold to be his servant.
He brought him from minding the ewes
to become the shepherd of his people.
And he shepherded them with all his heart
and guided them with skillful hand.

Psalm 78

In the same psalm David writes of the tallest trees growing near Israel and about the wildlife he knew so well.

The Lord's trees—the cedars of Lebanon
which he planted, are green and leafy.
Birds build their nests in them.
The stork makes her home at their very top.

High hills are the haunt of the mountain goat,
and boulders the badger's refuge.
You have made the moon to measure the year
and taught the sun where to set.
When you make darkness it is night,
all the beasts of the forest come out.
The young lions roar for prey,
seeking their food from God.
When you make the sun rise, they slink away
to rest in their lairs.
But men come out to work
until evening.
Countless are the things you have made, O Lord.
You have made all by your wisdom
and the earth is full of your creatures,
beasts great and small.
All of them look up to you,
waiting to be fed at the proper time.
What you give them, they take.
When you open your hand, they eat their fill.
When you hide your face, they are restless and troubled.
When you take their breath away, they weaken.
But when you breathe into them again, they recover.
You give new life to earth.

Psalm 104

David could be jealous, wanting what others had or did. He wrote how his life was like that of a rope climber, struggling to move up from bad to good. If he failed, he would fall into the open pit below.

My feet had almost slipped,
my foothold almost lost,
when sinners' boasts made me envious.
I saw how rich they were,
without pain or suffering,
sleek and sound in body,
as if without trouble or care.
Pride is their jeweled collar,
and violence the robe that wraps them.
Their eyes are set in folds of fat.
Whatever they say is mean and nasty.
How could they get so rich
when they are so bad?

Psalm 73

In another song, David sounds as though he had fallen into the pit at the bottom of the rope before getting help.

I waited, waited for the Lord.
He bent down and heard my cry
and brought me out of the muddy pit,
out of the mire and the clay.

He set my feet on a rock
and gave me firm footing
and a new song in my mouth,
a song of praise to our God.

Psalm 40

Sometimes when David felt lonely, he would take up his harp and sing.

How long, O Lord, will you forget all about me?
How long will you hide your face from me?
How long must I feel sadness in my soul,
grief in my heart, day and night?
See me and answer me, O Lord my God.

Psalm 13

Just as soon as he had asked for this help, David felt better. God had heard his song.

I trust in your true love.
My heart will be happy,
for you have set me free.
I will sing to the Lord, who has given me all I hoped for.

Psalm 13

David could write songs about doors and rocks as if they were more than wood and stone. He made them seem alive. One of the Psalms is about the powerful walls and gates of a city, thick and strong enough to protect the people within from any enemy.

Lift up your heads, you gates.
Lift yourselves up, you everlasting doors,
so the king of glory may come in.
Who is the king of glory?
The strong and mighty Lord.
The Lord mighty in battle.
Lift up your heads, you gates.
Lift them up, you everlasting doors,
that the king of glory may come in.

Psalm 24

When the children of Israel left their years of hard labor in Egypt, the Red Sea parted so that they could cross the waters as if on dry land, on their way to freedom and safety. David loved singing of this great escape, telling how God saved his people, the sons of Joseph and Jacob, freeing them from Egyptian slavery, under Moses's leadership.

The waters saw you, O God.
They saw you and swirled in fear.
The ocean was troubled to its depths.

Clouds poured water, and skies thundered.
Your arrows flashed here and there.
The sound of your thunder was in the whirlwind.
Your lightning lit the world,
as the earth shook and quaked.
Your path was through the sea,
your way through great waters.
And man could see your footsteps.
You guided your people like a flock of sheep,
under the hand of Moses and Aaron.

Psalm 77

David sang of the seven plagues God sent to the Egyptians, so they would let the children of Israel go. The Lord spoiled the Egyptians' water; sent flies and frogs and locusts to ruin their harvests, hailstones to kill the vines and the figs, even sickness to kill the firstborn Egyptian sons.

[God] led his own people,
like sheep, like a flock in the wilderness.
He lead them to safety and they were not afraid,
and the sea closed over their enemies.
He brought them to his holy mountain.

Psalm 78

That escape to freedom, from Egypt to the promised land, was one of David's favorite adventures. He may have remembered earlier songs, heard at home or in the temple, telling the same great story of Moses leading his people out of slavery. David sang it repeatedly, as if to remind himself that the Lord cared, that God was with him. Wherever he might be, whatever he might do, David would always be saved.

When Israel came out of Egypt,
and Jacob from a people of strange speech,
Judah became his new home, Israel his kingdom.
The sea looked and ran away.
The river Jordan turned back.
The mountains skipped like rams,
the hills like young sheep.
What was it, sea? Why did you run?
Jordan, why did you turn back?
Why, mountains, did you skip like rams?
And you, hills, like young sheep?
Dance, O earth, in the presence of the Lord.
Before the God of Jacob,
who turned the rock into a pool of water,
and the granite cliff into a fountain.

Psalm 114

In David's time, most people, like the Egyptians, believed in many gods; gods for rain and for sun, for corn and for blood, for life and for death. Their statues were carved of stone or wood, often beautifully painted and jeweled, and loved as we love the Lord. The Jews called these gods "false gods" or idols, and instead believed in one God. He was never to be shown in any statue or picture.

One of David's songs tells about the many people near Israel who were puzzled, wondering who the Jews' God might be since no pictures or statues of him could be found.

So why do the peoples ask,
"Where then is their God?"
Our God is in high heaven;
he does whatever pleases him.
Their idols are silver and gold,
made by the hands of men.
They have mouths but cannot speak,
and eyes that cannot see.
They have ears that cannot hear,
and noses that cannot yet smell.
With their fingers they cannot touch.
Their makers grow to be like them,
and so do all those who believe in them.

Psalm 115

Law is the heart of the Bible. To be fair and good, to follow the rules given in God's Commandments, to keep his word and love our family and neighbors, to care for the poor, these are the most important things for us to do. David knew that, but like most of us, found these rules hard to keep, breaking the Commandments as well as following them. He loved the laws even when he could not obey them. He praised the laws as God's greatest gift.

God's law is perfect.
His teaching never fails,
and makes the simple wise.
His rules are right:
They make us happy.
His commandments are so clear,
they shine.
God's laws are better than gold—
lots of it—
sweeter than syrup, or honey from the comb.

Psalm 19

Your hands moulded me and made me what I am:
Show me how I may learn your commandments.
O how I love your law!
I study it all day long.
Your commandments are mine forever.
With their help I am wiser than my enemies,

34

and know more than my teachers.
They make me wise more than the old,
because I follow your rules.
Your word is a lamp to guide my feet.
It lights my way.
Let the music of your promises be on my tongue,
for your commandments are justice itself.
I have strayed like a lost sheep.
Come search for your servant,
for I have not forgotten your commandments.
Hear Lord, my plea for fairness.
Bend down to hear me, listen to my words.
Show me how wonderful your true love can be.
Keep me the apple of your eye.
Hide me in the shadow of your wings,
from the wicked in my way.
The enemy is like a lion on the prowl,
like a young lion ready to pounce.
Rise, Lord, meet him face to face.
And bring him down.

Psalm 119

Not always a forgiving or gentle man, David was often
angry. A fighter, he cursed his enemies, hating those who
had once been his friends for lying about him. He asked
God to punish them, to bring terrible ruin, not only to them,
but to their wives and children.

O God who I praise, be silent no more,
for wicked men have lied to my face
and surrounded me with words of hate.
They have attacked me without reason,
accusing me though I've done no wrong.
They have repaid me with evil for good,
giving hatred in return for my love.

Psalm 109

David sang of such an enemy:

May his days be few;
may his hoarded wealth fall to another!
May his children be fatherless,
his wife soon a widow!
May his children be vagabonds and beggars,
driven from their homes!
May the money-lender take all that he owns,
and strangers seize his earnings!
May none remain loyal to him,
and none have mercy on his fatherless children!

Psalm 109

How could David have hated a man so much? Because
this man's lies and thanklessness had hurt him so much.
In the same song he wrote how badly he felt—miserable,

hungry, and lost. He did not know where or who he was.

I fade like a passing shadow,
I am shaken off like a locust.
My knees are weak with fasting
and I am getting far too thin, without eating.
I have become the victim of my enemies' taunts;
when they see me they toss their heads.
Let those who lie about me be clothed in their bad deeds,
wrapped in their shame like a cloak!
Then I will raise my voice to praise God!
For he stands at the poor man's side
to save him from his enemies.

Psalm 109

Comparing himself with those who lied about him,
David wrote:

Your lying tongue is as sharp as a razor.
You love evil and not good,
falsehood, not speaking the truth;
cruel gossip you love and mean talk.
So may God pull you down to the ground,
sweep you away, leave you ruined and homeless,
uprooted from the land of the living.

Psalm 52

Unlike that cruel man, David wrote:

I am like a spreading olive tree in God's house,
for I trust in his true love forever and ever.

Psalm 52

Many of the later psalms use words from army life; they tell of winning in the battlefield. David had become a great warrior. Sometimes he wrote as though he were arguing with God, as if he were trying to get a friend to come in on his side of a fight, making his friend angry and excited so that he would help.

Rise up, O God, fight for your side;
remember how brutal men tease you all day long.
You can't ignore the shouts of your enemies. . . .

Psalm 74

So David wrote of the Lord as a soldier as well as a judge.

God in heaven is my shield,
who saves men of honest heart.
God is a just judge;
every day he wins over the raging enemy.
He sharpens his sword,
strings his bow and makes it ready.

He has prepared his deadly shafts,
and tipped his arrows with fire.

Psalm 7

David sang about how God taught him to be a great
soldier and conqueror.

Blessed is the Lord, my rock,
who trains my hands for war,
my fingers for battle;
my help that never fails, my fortress,
my strong tower and my refuge,
my shield in which I trust;
he who puts nations under my feet.
I will sing a new song to you, O God,
psalms to the music of a ten-stringed lute.
O God who gave victory to kings
and freedom to your servant David,
rescue me from the cruel sword.
Snatch me from the power of foreign foes,
whose every word is false
and all their oaths lies.

Psalm 144

David's later songs told of life as both shepherd and warrior, combining fear and heroism, weakness with strength.

To you, O Lord, I call.
You are my rock.
Hear my cry.
Blessed be the Lord,
for he has heard my cry for mercy.
The lord is my strength, my shield.
My heart leaps for joy,
and I praise him with all of me.
O save your people and bless them.
Shepherd them and carry them forever.

Psalm 28

David's happiest soldier songs are those that add love to the warrior's force.

I love you, Lord, you are my strength;
my stronghold, my fortress, my champion.
God, you are my rock, where I find shelter;
my shield, my mountain refuge, my tower.

Psalm 18

He knew the life of the sailor as well as the soldier, singing:

Some go to sea in ships,
and earn their living on the wide waters.
They have seen how God works,
and his strange deeds.
The storm winds rise at his command,
lifting the waves high.
Raised heavenward, then plunged to the depths,
sailors toss to and fro.
In danger, they reel and stagger drunkenly,
all their knowledge of the sea useless.
So they call to the Lord for help,
and he brings them to safety.
The storm sinks to a murmur,
and the waves of the sea are stilled
as God guides the glad sailors to harbor.

Psalm 107

David could paint pictures with words as he sang of the wonders of God.

O Lord, you are great indeed,
clothed in majesty and splendor,
and wrapped in a robe of light.
You have spread out the heavens like a tent
and on the waters laid the beams of your pavilion.
You make your chariot from clouds,

you ride on the wings of the wind,
you make the winds your messengers
and flames your servants.
You fixed the earth so firmly,
it can never be shaken.
The waters lie over it like a cloak,
even above the mountains.
But at your rebuke they run,
at the sound of thunder rushing away,
flowing over the hills,
pouring into the valleys,
to their chosen places,
never covering the earth again.

Psalm 104

When David became king of Israel and founder of the
new Jerusalem, he sang of the kind of man he should be.

My heart is not proud,
I look down on no one.
I don't meddle with what
I can't understand.
No; I know who I am.
Humble as a baby,
still clinging to his mother.

Psalm 131

When he was old and had been the king of Israel for a long time, David still called to God, praising him and often asking for help.

Show me favor, O God, and save me.
Hurry to help me, O Lord.
May all my enemies be defeated,
and those who love to hate me
fall back, powerless.
Let those who long for your help sing,
"All glory to God!"
I am poor and needy, O Lord.
Hasten to my help.
Don't delay.
O God, you have taught me since boyhood;
all my life I have sung of your wonderful works.
Now that I am old and my hair is gray,
don't forget me.

Psalm 71

Singing near the end of his long life, David remembered:

Tears may come at night
and joy in the morning.
You have turned me from sadness
to dancing,

taken off my rags
and clothed me with joy.

Psalm 30

No one wrote sadder songs than David. When he sang
of the flood, he meant all the troubles that were pouring in
on him.

Save me, from the flood,
for the waters have risen up to my neck.
I am sinking in the deep mud, without a foothold,
as I am swept into deep water and the flood
carries me away.
I am sick of crying out, my throat is sore,
my eyes grow dim as I wait for God's help.

Psalm 69

David felt better when he told God about his thoughts
and feelings, even if they were cruel. He didn't spend too
much time thinking before he did what he wanted. Sometimes what he wanted wasn't good. That brought sadness as
well as joy. David is all of us, at our best and worst: jealous
and loving, mean and caring, brave and weak. So he prayed
to God, singing to him, asking for his forgiveness.

From the depths I call to you, O Lord.
Hear my cry.

48

Listen to my plea for mercy.
If you, O God, counted all our sins,
who could ever hold up his head?
But you are forgiving.
That is why we love you.
I wait for the Lord.
My soul waits for God
more eagerly than watchmen for the morning.

Psalm 130

David knew the world was always changing; nothing stays just the same. Changes could be for the better or for the worse. He wrote:

God turns rivers into desert,
and springs of water into thirsty ground.
He turns fruitful land into salt waste,
because the men who live there are so wicked.
Wilderness he changes into standing pools,
and parched lands into springs of water.
There he gives the hungry a home,
and they build themselves a city to live in;
they sow fields and plant vineyards
and reap a fruitful harvest.

Psalm 107

He told God just how it felt to reach the end of his days.

Listen to my prayer,
and when I call, answer me soon.
For my days vanish like smoke
and my body is burnt up as
in an oven.
I am weak, shriveled like dry grass.
I can't find the strength to eat.
Wasting away, I groan aloud,
my skin hanging from my bones.
I am like a desert owl in the wilderness,
an owl that lives among ruins.
Thin and meager, I hoot in solitude,
like a bird fluttering on the rooftop.

Psalm 102

Under David's son, wise King Solomon, the great temple of Jerusalem was completed. Soon people from all over the land of Israel came to see the city and its greatest wonder, the beautiful new temple. But long before it was finished, Jerusalem was a great and holy city where people came to see the palace and many other buildings, pilgrims from far away places to pray or wonder at these marvels. David wrote songs for these travelers to the new city that he had built.

I rejoiced when they said to me,
"Let us go to the house of the Lord."
Now we stand within your gates,
O Jerusalem,
where people come together as one,
where the tribes of the Lord come, to give him thanks.
In Jerusalem are set the thrones of justice,
the thrones of the house of David.
Pray for the peace of Jerusalem:
"May those who love you prosper;
peace be within your ramparts
and prosperity within your palaces."
For my brothers and my friends
I will say, "Peace be within you."
For the house of the Lord our God,
I will pray for you.

Psalm 122

Of his many deeds, David was proudest of founding Jerusalem as Israel's new capital—the city of Zion. In one psalm he reminded God never to forget how and when and why he wanted Jerusalem built.

O Lord, remember David in the time of his troubles,
how he promised to the Mighty one of Jacob:
I will not enter my house

nor get onto my bed,
I will not close my eyes in sleep
until I find a home for the Lord,
a dwelling place for the Mighty One of Jacob.

Psalm 132

What David meant by a home for the Lord was the
placing of the tabernacle—the Ark with its two tables of the
law, in the great new temple.

David recalled how God had promised him that he and
his sons would be rulers if they followed His word, how the
Lord would feed the city's needy, clothe her priests, and
bless David's descendants, crowning him, and shaming his
enemies. His song reminded his listeners:

For the Lord has chosen Zion
and desired it for his home.
"This is my resting place forever.
Here I will make my home, that is what I want."

Psalm 132

Among the towering columns of Jerusalem's new temple, the songs first sung by the shepherd boy in the Lord's
praise were heard once again. But now, with far more than
a small harp and a single voice, David also wrote new songs
for the new temple, whose curved ceiling—the vault—looked
like heaven's. One of these was the last of his Psalms.

O praise the Lord.

O praise God in his holy place.

Praise him in the vault of heaven, the vault of his power.

Praise him for his mighty works.

Praise him for his immeasurable greatness.

Praise him with trumpet fanfares.

Praise him upon lute and harp.

Praise him with tambourines and dancing.

Praise him with the flute and strings.

Praise him with the clash of cymbals.

Let everything that has breath praise the Lord!

O praise the Lord.

Psalm 150

But such splendid songs, played in the great temple of Jerusalem by many singers and many other musicians, were no more joyous than those of the little boy, singing all alone under the moon and stars, with only his sheep to keep him company.

ABOUT THE AUTHOR

Colin Eisler, the distinguished art historian, is Robert Lehman Professor of Fine Arts at the Institute of Fine Arts of New York University. He is the author of *Cats Know Best* (Dial), illustrated by Lesley Anne Ivory, and his many publications include *The Genius of Jacopo Bellini, Paintings in the Hermitage,* and *Dürer's Animals.* Mr. Eisler is on the exhibitions committee of the Jewish Museum of New York, and also teaches at the Jewish Theological Seminary. He was a Lenten Lecturer at the Madison Avenue Presbyterian Church in New York City. Mr. Eisler lives in New York City.

ABOUT THE ARTIST

Jerry Pinkney is an award-winning illustrator of children's books and has also been honored for the body of his work with a Citation for Children's Literature from Drexel University, and with the David McCord Children's Literature Citation from Framingham State College. He has also received the Alumni Award for 1992 from the Philadelphia College of Art and Design. Mr. Pinkney's work has been exhibited at the Indianapolis Museum of Art, Cornell University, and at the University of Delaware; a traveling exhibition of his paintings has been shown at the Philadelphia Afro-American Historical and Cultural Museum, the Schomburg Center for Black Culture in New York City, and at the University at Buffalo, where Mr. Pinkney is Visiting Professor in the Department of Art.

Jerry Pinkney lives with his wife Gloria in Croton-on-Hudson, New York.